HARSH BASWAL

The everlasting love of a dying hope.

Night will weave another story, a rug that won't be enough.

I need the sky.

Some fire from the womb of this earth and a piece of moon.

The piece that hangs by my windows while I sip coffee from your cup.

CONTENTS

☐ *PROLOGUE*

☐ *ADDICTED*

☐ *AFZAN AND ENCOUNTER*

☐ *GAY TOP MEN*

☐ *I AM GAY*

☐ *NON ACCEPTANCE*

☐ *BETRAYED*

☐ *STRUGGLES TO COUNT*

☐ *SYED*

PROLOGUE

This book will give you a glimpse about the lives of LGBTQIA+ members in the country.

These encounters not just only make you aware the kind of situations we as a community is facing in the country but at the same time also entertain you with mixed emotions. Being the second largest populas country of the world and the great largest diversity in terms of the cultures and the largest democracy of the world , it is quite sure for all of us to know that it then must be having a great number of LGBT population in the country but apart from the image of being a welfare state this country doesn't provide such safeguards which make it stand in the list of very promising nations in terms of human rights .

Actually the situation here is not just always critical only for homosexual peoples but also for the minorities in the country , it took 75 years after the country independence from the british to legal gay sex in the country , almost every day people treat us like hangers , slut's and prostitutes !

why we are not respected as equal citizens of this country ?

why there are no safeguards for us?

Apart from the transgender people why we don't have marriage rights ?

why in every sphere of life in this country we were denied justice and our independency?

The encounters which I had experienced and am sharing with the audience have so many faces with it just like the American sociologist once comprehend that whenever a person express something it always *have many faces which not just tells you the story of the single person but also reflects so many hidden contents from it which the reader have to find out from its own consciousness.*

Every story is different from the other story of the book so as to open a vastness of assumptions for the readers , in the end of every chapter there I left with a thought for the readers of how the situations of the people can be changed either by their own effort or through the joint efforts of the community peoples.

The last and the most important things about this book is for its search for acceptance .

ADDICTED

"No two fingers of a hand is of same size and similarly no two persons are same and this is totally similar with addictions"

some are addicted to drugs !

some are addicted to robbery!

but I am addicted with sex "gay sex"!

I was 14 when I found my interest are different from others , and as students of my age were looking for girls , I was looking for boys but the difference here comes that they were looking girls of same age for having friendship with them but I was looking for boy's , men's older than me not for any friendship but for sex. When I found I got addicted with it at that time I was already 18 and in my first year of graduation , but this addiction takes it's next level and experience it's peak time during these years only. There are encounters with many people's here by people i actually mean people : "men's , boy's , trans , neutral's , sides"and many others. this addiction of mine first fulfilled by my own uncle but soon and after when I got bored with him , then I started searching for another unmarried , married , or carefree boy's , sometimes I found them and many a times they found me , those days I don't have any cell with me and this is the reason of me getting engaged with boys of my own locality and this is how I got my names , after doing sex or getting done with boy's of my own community and locality , I always tell them not to tell this to anybody but as always happens they used to narrate the whole wild things either to their friend or to anyone who's close to them . earlier such wild narrations of me and their intimate coitus stories had created problems for me as if whenever I go for local market's or for doing other works nearby my neighboring area's too these people started following me and whenever and wherever they got chance they started demanding me pleasure's of bed at a cost of maintaining my secret identity , after getting done with me they provoke their friends to make their heads also count into this list and some where this is also the reason of me getting addicted to this "sex".

I saw this time period of my world as 2 sided :

1. the one side where I was facing problems with this situation and secound I was getting my demands fulfilled through the tastes of different boy's and men's , at a certain phase now after so many years of these budding roots of my taste I feel that at that particular point of time I was serving as a common sex worker for the community but with the cost of maintaining my own sacredness.

One such incident which had provoked many to having me on their diet of bed on that's day was of 2016, I was pursuing my higher studies , and since I am from a low middle class family it's very easy for people who were rich to gain control over me and this thought really got's it's shape during the winter of 2016. I was feeding my animals when a boy named shanker living near my locality comes next to a bench near me and started staring me , he got to know about me and my sexuality through ravi who's my uncle in relation but as in my story where blood relations are more dangerous than enemies to destroy other member's he is just a community named uncle , I had never done sex with ravi neither with any of his brother upto now but I don't know from where or with whom he *got to know about me, I know Shankar by his father because his father was a government employee and his brother a merchant and his family have a good name within the caste and locality. at the time when I was feeding my goats ravi came next to me and slowly whispered in my ears that "Shankar was calling you" I had heard about ravi from some of my locality queen "transgenders" that he works a s a broker and always took advantage of those poor people usually families having more girls and after a quick short supply of money help to the kin's family he sold that individual to the nearby brothel of our locality " basically my caste is touchable dalit but our situation in the country is similar to the untouchable Dalits – most of the families in our community survived hand to mouth, the nature of family is patriarchal and children's usually grow up by seeing domestic violence as the regular episode of their daily dharavaik" first I ignore him because I had heard many things about his brother who's mentally unstable and with his father too who had several times cheated on his mother and even about Shankar that he is a drug addict and had rapped a child earlier and was earlier remanded by the Bombay high court under the posco act at that time I didn't know anything about the posco act nor whether these controversies are true or just stories for demeaning his family. After a few minutes thinking and taking these instances into consideration I went to the bench where he was sitting I went there along with my goats so that no one really understands whether I was talking with him or with ravi and thought that the people will assume as if I was making my goats graze their leaves. At that time I was not cleaned because I had not taken bath and after cleaning the goats the darbha{house} my situation of clothes and body becames more messed like the galliyan of madangiri, making me watch he told me in a very demanding manner that he wants to have sex with me and so do ravi, Shankar is from a Brahmin family and at this point of time I didn't know his intentions or whether he believes in caste system or not, from the onset of my childhood I had seen even in the national capital territory of india that even after things and quotes like "untouchability is a sin, it's a crime, its inhuman"people doesn't discard it wholeheartedly and the actual ground reality will never be realized till the time when again elections will approach and for not the gods sake but for the vote bank sake we will be counted as a part of this indian population, I know brahmins have always been demanding and even they are more clever enough so as the subdued the real natives of the indian subcontinent and maintained their state{dasyus} poorer than their earlier hunter and gather forfathers . I found this very strange because earlier I was the one who chooses with whom I want to have sex and many a times I even decide the duration when the other person is not good at it , I directly took all my goats from there to my area of park and tied them to the rope ,in a gesture of nodding I replied him in a NO.*

But as I had already mentioned he is a rich men and can afford anything by paying its price and for a below poverty line person like me it's easy for him to get me under his control want me either by directly harassing me or by paying my price to me .

After a week pass or so I realized that someone was following me towards my way to school then my way to home my way to field when I go there to work , and many a times my way to work in the small shop of ours , one day when I was closing my shop I saw a hand grabed my mouth from the back and pulled me in the opposite direction of mine suddenly I realized that someone had now tied my legs and hands too and then my eyes so that I wasn't able to see who that person is , but when I started weeping from the open mouth I realized that I was pinched at my face and that too by two different persons this I got sure from the sensation of the punch from two different directions and then a cloth was crowd in my mouth which starts bleeding though , I even heard boys voices not of two boys but many laughing and calling me by different names one word which I get to adapt from my sinful childhood is chakka and meetha-paan , I don't know by what time I lost my consciousness and when I get up I found myself in a high rised building roof and found so person over my body fucking me , he was taking poppers and then I turned my head and found that all other boys by and large 15 in number were dancing at the same roof just next to the fucking spot of mine , when the boy high on drugs came to realize that I now got my consciousness soon covers his face with his own kurta which he was wearing and not letting the other persons of his group seeing his small dick but he didn't stopped fucking me till the time he discharged all his energy in my ass. After he Step up from the place now another men comes over me I acted as if still not in a state to rebel but when I found it painful to get fucked by him I moaned and there he concluded that I am conscious well enough to remember their names and faces , he called ravi which was sitting just next before shankar he was that much drugged that even after calling 10 to 12 times he took 5 minutes to reach the spot now I know why it's so , because he and Shankar was also fucking a lesbian girl forcefully which they brought here just as they brought me , when he came , that person started shouting and started saying awful things which not even the queen says in our slum houses when they came for badhai . when he saw that I saw him he started giving me drug injections but when I rebelled forcefully he resigned because now he was more drunk on the free rum of Shankar , I without looking at any other point at the place started collecting my clothes and suddenly grasped by a tight manly hand who twisted my ankles and when I shouted someone slept on my face making my bleeding nose run with more blood than earlier and started rapping me in front my all others present there , not even a single person from that assembly of young crooked people came forward for my protection the thing which I was hearing was just sounds of weeping of that lesbian girl whom I know because she stays in my locality and was a jain .

After he got done from me he threw 500 rs/- at my face and said this is what you had never seen just take this and leave our place , he even blamed me of ruining his party , when after wearing my clothes I refused the 500 note and said to Shankar that I will be going to tell all this instances first to my family and second to his father and especially his orthodox mother everyone started laughing present there but only the two young boys present there at the last row seemed most discomfort with such thoughts of mine , then quickly Shankar again ripped my clothes and started beating me with all he have in his hand and started abusing me by my caste and sexuality after around 30 minutes of hustle and bustle fighting he let me go freely but without my clothes and said this is my punishment of even thinking of making him punish either through the society rules or by the constitution , by even not listening what he said I get out of the roof by the stairs and not by the lift because of camera service available in the lift at that moment I didn't have even a single cloth on my body .

when I got on the street I saw some kotti's were doing dhandha{prostitution} along with their gurus . when they noticed me one of the kotti came urgently running having a duppata of her guru in his hand and covered me in that by looking at his face I found that this person is non other than my own childhood friend madhav whose parents abandon him when he tells them about their sexuality and desires "madhav belongs to the baniya caste and what he told me at the day when he was leaving his home that in their caste such desires and free expressions are restricted and people saw them sinful – by knowing all this from madhav that day almost the whole night I imagined what happened with me and my family when my untouchable community came to know about me though".

By looking at me madhav started crying and all the gurus surrounded me not letting the other people seeing my face and giving their services a short period of hault , there then comes bijli in the scene who used to head the queens and kottis dhandha in our locality , I had heard about her from all my relatives that she knows even the commissioner of our province and even gave him with services whenever required at the same time gave monthly to police men's so that they didn't interrupt in the functioning of their kotha and services!

Bijli in a very harsh and hard tone asked me about who did all this to me she is in a hurry of asking me because I was the one who was causing her loss of revenue by not letting their girls attention away from me , usually when it comes to LGBT persons in the city , it looks as a daily routine of harassment in many a ways which even includes rape and murder after getting angry at my silence she left me alone with her workers by giving them 15 minutes ultimatum of getting back to work , madhav who used to operate from the home left my hand into another kotthi hand rushed to his kotha house and bring a Dettol jelly cream and some clothes of her for me to wear.

I was silenced from the time I left my consciousness to the time I get it in a state I wished no one would love to get to , then after having me with some parathas in my hand he left me in the way to my home because now rest had comes to an end and its my hard time to explore what will be my next step .

Usually mostly hetrosexual men's either becamas kotti's when they were rapped or they started living dual lives even generate dual personalities within them which is different when it comes to gays and transgenders .

After that current event of morose rape I went upstairs to my building {my real house} with great care so that not even the dogs sleeping on the streets notices me and started making sound I saw the time it's just 1 at night and my parents were at the small railing of our house to look for me , I saw them they were looking at the railing time by time and turn and turn this created another problem for me that I was wearing clothes which are not even mine and are very feminine if my parents came to know it "the rape event" I don't know how will they react to and what if their dignity was at stake just because of me , my desires , pleasures and because of an never explained tragedy !.

I went at home when I found that now no one is looking from the railing and now its really safe for me to get changed easily and quickly without anyone's notice , I executed the plan very well and by some sort of noise which I had created when I was bathing and crying I heard some foot steps coming nearer to the bathroom and then I shut mum and realized that It's really not the hard time of crying but to create a story for the family members for where I have been so long without even giving any information or giving my unpresence to anyone's notice , I quietly and quickly took the bath changed the clothes and threw madhav's clothes the roof next to my house building so that no one founds it in my house and suspects any one of us specially me and quietly took the food from the cooker and ate it silently and then went to sleep next to my mother , the next morning what I found that no one was interested in asking me where I was the last night for so long not even my own parents , but found the regular duties of mine in my head told by my mom when she was leaving for the field work in a farm .

first I thought this as an nightmare but then - I when after getting over all my household works I started suspecting and intterogating things which I did earlier night like throwing madhav clothes at next roof to my building I found those there only and this made's me more scared and my mind more proximate with vivid thoughts like what happens if my parents came to know about that last night , what if our caste members came to know about this?

do they also made us jaat bahar? just as the madhav caste had done with him and many such imaginative things.

Todays reality with this chapter lies truly untouched till this date of time and year because only the time had passed for me but the image , the crime and the criminals were today also standing in front of me as respectful persons and entities and for them and this society now I am the dhabba{black spot} on and over their civilization which they fuck with due passion in dark but denied respect and dignity in every sphere of culture , tradition and life !.

AFZAN AND ENCOUNTER

"Encounters are what which we all have , something exiting , interesting , which comes with a hope to find our real one. I never disagree on the fact that I didn't have any in my life till now but I agree that those which I have are more memorable than any other's. my list of encounters or meeting peoples is not a small one to remember and that's the reason I only remember the most touched one's from the hearts to bodies".

"The things which I always do care of before meeting to a particular person is:

where is the place where we are going to meet each other ?

is that person open about his life ? {usually in a conservative society like india , people are not much open about their personal lives , their way of living , and the persona of seeing the world} but if a person is , then he / she is looked with demeaning. It's a taboo in our country to being lived , loved , and prosper through a person's own choices.

What's his position {top, bottom, versatile} ?

Distance between my home and his place ?

Whether he lives alone or with family ?

And precautiones questions like such.

After knowing this much about a person can also be risky if the person have other intentions for you.

One day I was travelling in the metro from saket to race course ,this is the time when I was still in the final year of my school , I have to rise early around 5am in the morning because my school starts around 7am , I am very passionate about my studies and this is the reason why I had never take a leave all time in the final years of my schooling , race course is around 11 kilometers away from saket and this is the reason why I had to rise that much early even in the winters days as well when it was too dark to travel on the delhi metropolitan roads . I always used to take a bus first from madangir to saket metro station and then went for race course metro station and from that also I had to take a walk of around 2 km because of the security reasons in that area . the season in those days was foggy , misty ,winter and there was a huge accumulation of smog all over the old delhi and new delhi areas , through this much of smog one cannot see in a transparent way and because of this in those winter season days I usually took my bus around 5:30 am and be there in saket metro station around 5:40 am , at that early time of the day no one were there in the metro so I make myself comfortable in the vacant metro boggi's and travel.

The month was January and that day was an exception because it's not like the previous sole travelling days of mine , the exception comes in the metro in the form of a handsome brown boy, that boy entered from the malviya nagar metro station and I was already there in the metro, we both were really amazed by seeing a other person in the time of starting of the day but we don't talk with each other all around the journey from our source stations to destination stations we were just passing smiles to each others by looking at each other in frequent intervals range into each others face and sometimes body. Another exception which I got that sudden moment was we have similar destination stations when that person comes to know this through my presence in the metro's counter , he comes next to me and started taking my side on the conversation of changing my metro card , this made me laugh on the way he was talking to the encounter officer and watching me laugh on his thought provoking conversation with the officer , he suddenly with not wasting any more time asked my name and the truth is with not wasting any more time I also told him my name and this is how the conversation starts between us along the lines of delhi metro and in between the path of friendship. When we were entering into the exit gates he told me his name "AFZAN" then he started asking about me like:

Which school I was in ?

What subjects I was having ?

What are my interest ?

Which hobby I like the most ?

And the most important question which he asked was whether I am introvert or extrovert ?

I reacted very positively on all his questions instead of knowing that's he is a stranger and this was the first day of our meeting, without asking of mine he started telling me about his hometown which was gulmerg in Kashmir, about his family members and his hobbies which was to play basketball, he even told me about his work profile, he used to work in a coaching institute and was preparing for the civils exam, at that point of time I didn't understand how can be a person that much frank to a stranger or maybe I was thinking very much, AFZAN was handsome, he was struggling to maintain his rank in the civils exam, he was a successful trainer and teacher who was loved by many of his students and the most important thing about him was he was not shy and never feels uncomfortable in an orthodox society like india about his sexuality, the thing about that period was now for some people is normal but at that time the british imposed 377 was not repealed by the supreme court of india and that's why most of the LGBTQ persons at that particular period of time were not extrovert's or we can say doesn't feel viable in the society because of their tastes in bed, I was also that kind of a person, I was bullied a lot in my school days not by students but even by teachers. they used to call me with different names, there was a incident which happened with me when I was in my 9th standard, A boy always made fun of mine in the class during the recess time, during our games period and several times at different places within the day. One day he was punished by the principal because of his behavior towards me and other girls, during that whole punished time he was looking at me and after the end of the school we all went towards metro station because that was the only place from where other students got their buses but not the primary and junior school students that day is always like a normal day for me upto 3 pm when that boy along with some other boys struck my way to the metro and started beating me infront of all other students and when I was lying on the floor of the footpath and crying no other student or any other person came to help me even those students were cheering those boys and everybody have a different name for me, a girl comes forward first and gave me a title of gaysian, other boy from those in the gang gave me a tilte of brownie queen and then this ceremony started everybody started giving me names like : drag queen, grey queen, chicken queen, sausage jockey, unicorn, soy boy, tranny, ginger beer, queen princess and variations .that day the fact hurts me the most was "that even the teachers were looking at all this drama but no one from those also came forward to help me" this incident even scared me during my all years of *schooling and makes its place in a corner of my mind and somewhere in my soul which always used to point towards the weakness which I don't have and the rights which also at the same time I don't have at that point of my life. and now after 6 years of this incident , whenever I look back in the windows of the past memories now I realise how wrong those people were at that time and how wrong they will remain in their future prospects.*

AFZAN was not like me in his school days even after belonging to a muslim family , he told everything about his likes , dislikes and interest to his mother at the age of 15 , what afzan told me was-that his parents were very supportive towards him at every stage of his life and this is how I guess he gained courage to tell everybody everything about him because he knew that not every person and every child is not that lucky that he was. That day our chat took sudden turns when I took left and he took right for our destinations , after listening what afzan told about him I was very curious to know more about him but the sad part was that my school gets over in 2pm and his job in 4 pm and this 2 hour gap no one from both of us can resist because both of us have families and that was the final year of my schooling which means I have had to study a lot to gain a seat in delhi university and that's why I don't wait for him neither he waited for me the only time where we met was in the morning and that's for 40 minutes , where 20 minutes we were in the metro and 20 minutes we were with each other walking and talking. He told me many facts about Kashmir , I also know about Kashmir from different texts and books and even from our syllabus books but not in that much depth in which he knows and that's why I used to listen him all time from metro to changing of directions ,

one day there was winter rain the whole morning smog settled down a little and was giving the whole surrounding a pleasant and soothing smell of soil , that day I was a little late to catch my metro because the area of madangir is not having proper drainage facilities neither proper mettelled roads and this is the reason why being a part of delhi the national capital this area is only occupied by local merchants , weavers , students who want cheap accommodation and labour class workers , this area is not that developed as other areas of delhi and that's why during rainy seasons specially the roads became inaccessible and hard to approach. When I went into the saket metro station I found someone waiting for me that's actually not the person with whom I talk daily from source to destination, that person approaches me in a very obscure way, when I was putting my bag into the scanner table he grabbed my hand and said to me that "he want the whole truth right from the beginning otherwise he will be gonna destroy my life and became a threat for my family" after saying all this me I don't know where but he disappeared. I got scared from that incident very much that even after making my bag cheaked I decided not to go school at that day and then took my bag from the security guard and went to my home, I don't know actually whether at that day afzan was waiting for me or he just went for his work or whether he also took a leave that day, after that incident things became more obscure for me, the major reason for this unsettled state of mind were those men's statements with whom I met in the metro station that day, from the very next day we were having our holidays started for the prepration of our pre-boards exams, those days of mine were among the worst days of my life because there was a thought of threat in my mind without even knowing the reason for it and at the same time I have to prepare for my examinations along with all other home responsibilities, in those days after 3 or 4 days of that threating call I forgot everything what that stranger told to me and I started my prepration for exams, after 12 days when our winter break got over we had our first exam actually that day before going to school I guess every classmate of mine was thinking of clearing that exam but I was thinking of not meeting that person again in metro or in other place, after gaining courage by touching my mother's feet I went to school just like I really do first the bus and second the metro. when I went in the vacant metro I feel very relaxed because I didn't saw that person in the cheking counter but I was afraid because there were almost 7 stations more and 20 minutes walk to my destination but there was a hope to meet afzan so that I can share that all with him, actually I was thinking a lot with so much characters in my mind but that day neither I met afzan nor that threating person but :

 the thing which I received gained a prominent space in my heart and gave me a lesson for life, that day I got a letter from another men who was waiting for me at that place where I took left and afzan right that men didn't show his face to me but he pulled me towards him and gave a letter in my hand, I saw tears in his eyes and was feeling his slow and warm breath coming towards my mouth at that point I am sure now that he was afzan but I didn't understand why he was covering his face and why he was crying, he kissed me gently on my lips with scarf on his face and pushed me left which was really my direction, when I managed to collect my material along with his letter from the footpath I saw no one there , I didn't follow the right direction and went in the left because I have to give my exam , I put his letter under my sweater in my shirt's pocket and went in the school to gave my exam , after the exam the hall becames really noisy because all students were having their lunch some of them were even discussing their paper , some others were gossiping and some just went for a walk in the school's ground . I don't want to take that paper out from my pocket in front of all these students because if anyone from those specially boys came to know about this then they will directly hand over that to the principal and I don't want that to happen with me because I was also not familier with the letter's content and that's why instead of having curiosity to read that I took a safe side I went into the music room of my school where no one except the old music teacher comes , because of having great skills in vocal music I got permission to use the instruments of that room and get entry into the room with the principal , I went inside into the room turn on the lights and take out the letter to read .

The letter had its starting in a very good approaching way just like afzan approaches :

"my sweet little dear harsh"

I know that you are the only person which will understand the situation through which I am going , you and me have similarities , you and me have love for each other , you and me waited for so long to be loved , you and me have dreams for changing or reforming society , but now it's not you and me only you because this is the last time when you saw me alive I don't know whether you have heard about the ISIS or not but now the truth is I am not a struggler who was preparing for indian civils exam but I worked as an agent of this terror outfit organization , I know you must having a thought in your mind that why I joined it instead of going for some decent job , harsh sweetheart the government is not listening what I want them to listen , they are just making assumptions "I just wana make it clear to you that I didn't personally join this terror outfit because of my religion but of my sexuality" I am a homosexual in this diversified country and a criminal in the eyes of the constitution and governance , I didn't have my rights protected nor do I have any financial assistance from my family because this time also I lied to you the actuality is that my family abandon me when they came to know about my preffrences , harsh I want you to study and achieve what I was not able to just promise me one thing that you will be having patience because it will take time for societies to evolve and change .

I love you ……….. your afzan.

This chapter always remains very close to my soul because this is the first time when I got my love and lost him too now I really regret of not chasing him in the right direction and of not reading that letter at that moment only , I don't know what afzan is for the people of the nation but for me he is my first lover and a person who was from his very childhood denied his liberty , privacy , dignity and most importantly basic fundamentals rights which today make him a terrorist yes I'm right I saw him once again when I was in my final year of graduation but not as afzan but as an terrorist named habul who's pictures along with his fake name and rewarding amount had been pasted on the outer walls of the metro station gate.

today I don't know where he is?

what he is doing?

But I want him to read this and come back to me to india because now the laws have been changed somewhat in positive direction for homosexuals and I really want him to remind his own thoughts that society takes time to evolve .

GAY TOP MEN

After one month this will be the second time when we will be going to meet each other again , the first meeting was a little uncomprehensive in many ways because earlier when I was there at the bus stand when it was my first day to meet him I got a little angry on him because instead of coming to the bus stand he told me that he will be going to give me directions to come to his apartment . when I said to him that I will go back to my place , he just got some energy I don't know from where he *got that and he said to me wait at the church which is near to that bus stand after a little negotiations I agree , near that church was a boy who was trying to stand by his own but he was facing some kind of problem after getting near to that boy I found that he was injured from his knee and after talking to him I suggested him to go to the nearby hospital suddenly that boy asked me , are you waiting for someone?*

I replied him by simply nodding my head , 2/3 minutes later he came after looking at me for about 1 minute he pulled me towards him and quietly whispered in my ears wanna have ……. I smiled and then we went for his apartment , in the walk for that apartment we talked about our interests , our future goals , about our family and most importantly about our prefferences in sex he told me that he is top and he knows about me that I am versatile , after geeting into his apartment I saw many states of things within different corners of the room , he quitly come next to me and said this is the reason why I am cancelling todays meet but I kissed his forehead and told him that I will help you in making your arrangements . he told me that he recently shifted to that place and after 1 month her mother will be coming to see him , after having some softdrinks , we started kissing each other the pull and the holding of my body is so hard that I can even feel his fingers on my waist , he then started licking my neck and suddenly he becomes so passionate that he take over all my clothes and so of his . he comes next to me and as he always does again whispered in my ears " lets take the things to the next level " and as I always does just nodded my head in a yes after that he kissed me so hard that even the exhaled breath of mine he can feel and so do I feel his , he grabed me in his arms , lift me in his hands and then take me over to his room , on his bed after looking at me for a while he again comes next to my ears and asked me whether I want to have intercourse or not I replied in a yes . his passion then touches to the next level and I guess this yes is what he is waiting for months , after having sex of around 2/3 times in that day , I feel totally in him but I don't know what he feels about me , he is 10 years older than me , worked in a IT company , leaved his hometown at the age of 20 because of his sexual prefferences , I don't know whats the story of that men because definitely at first hookup no one tells you about his whole life , the most answered questions during the time of gay hookups are whether both of them hygenic {means HIV negative} , their positions { are they top , bottom , versatile , or have sides } and their dick sizes but apart from all these talks one moment I stole from that men the time when I was talking to him and he kissed me at my cheeks and then sleep in my arms didn't even making me noticed him , after watching him sleeping , usually when gay boys have sex with bisexuals they never kissed them nor in their lips neither in their cheeks and forehead is just out of question and that's the reason why I stole that moment from that gay top men later around 7 in the evening I took my clothes wore them quietly take my bag and leaved his apartment .

I accept that such encounters now became a part of my life even people of my own group and family judge me when any of them came to know about this. But because I enjoyed it in this way only that's why I totally left it now in their hands either to judge or accept.

When I reached my home after having intense coitus with that men I literally can't stop thinking about him , but at the same time I even didn't know anything useful and important about him apart from his dick size and his intense look which he gave while fucking , these things and stuff in my head made me to call him once again , this is the same day when we meet but now the timings had changed it's 8 in the night and at this time I called him , he picked up the phone and started interviewing me thinking of an unknown person on the other side of the call but when I told him very politely about the day meeting he started laughing and even meanwhile in the discussion make fun of mine , in the end when he cut off the call ,

by my insistence gave me another appointment from the very next day in the morning to his house.

Because of the fact that my college is very near to this interesting men's house it was very easy for me to take a walk from my college to reach his apartment , in delhi we usually preffer to live in flats and apartments and not like rural areas where people usually believe to have as much large and open places they can get or occupy and after some time register them , at that day when I went for his apartment I saw two other persons were also coming from his house before I could get in there , I stopped at a little distance and saw all the drama happening slowly and with very care , those two persons were threatening him and he was giving them money upto that time period I didn't know why he was paying them and why they were threatening him.

When the boys went from his apartment after taking the money, I took 5 to 10 minutes to get in the top men's house. when I get in the house I saw him having drugs by seeing me at the gate first he shivered but at the very next moment he also offered me the drugs, after seeing such multiple sides of a person I got very scared and wants to take a leave from there but because I want to know the truth and the mystery of those two persons, I told him to sit on the chair next to him and bring him a glass of water then took off his clothes first and then mine and take him to the shower room where we both cleaned each other in between all this I really have so much curiosity of asking him so many questions but I took precautions because somewhere right now he was high on drugs, I ordered some pizza from the apartment's landline number and within 30 minutes I got my order when the lunch arrived {pizza in this case} he became a little sober and didn't want me to pay the bill but when I payed it, he insisted of sharing the whole bills into 2 halves, when I nodded a yes he kissed my forehead bring 2 glasses from the kitchen in whivh he generously poured wine and then served it delicately.

It's now 4 in the evening and I have had my class at 5:00pm so I thought taking leave from him, when I told him that I was leaving he closed the door and locked it and throw the keys above the shelf next to the kitchen room, by watching this I laughed and said to him why don't you tell me directly to stay and not to leave, he came next to me and as he does whispered in ears something sensual and then again we got into our moments.

After having done it 2 times in that day it's around 6 in the evening, we both were in bed, in the blanket, and kissing taking advantage of the moment I asked him about what I saw in the morning by listening this very quietly he get up and makes me too, at that point of time I thought he will threw me out from his house but the case is reversed he took my hands into his and asked me 2 simple questions :1. What kind of stuff I read the most ?

My answer is very quick with detailing's : I read love stories and by saying this I started telling him some of the love stories book's which I had read already and other's which I will be reading in this year or so.

he asked me.have you seen American gay web series "QUUER AS FOLK"?.

I replied in a yes by as usual nodding my head in a yes.

He said what is the similarity you got to know from 1. From your favoriote novel the boyfriend and 2. From queer as folk !

I got my question answered very efficiently and now all my queries have good solutions of them but I make him promise that from the next time he will not be having drugs just to pass his lonliness .

Actually the similarity is that in both the cases the author and the director shows that the main lead characters got their love who is 10 to 12 years smaller than the main lead and second before meeting their love both the characters does all kinds of stuffs so as to overcome from their emptiness and the answer why the 2 were asking him money is because he had borrowed some drugs from them without paying them the real amount on time .

We had talked 2 months before we had decided not to . the reasons are not so much metropolitan as the city is and this is how a gay top men got his position among the most remembered person in my life.

I'M GAY

Before the people accept me, it's me who had accepted myself the way actually I am.

I know I am different , I was different , and will remain the same as this being myself is not actually in my control, some people think that these are the habits which can be changed like : in a country of so much diversity people have different opinions about being a homosexual in the country," some thought that this is the western concept and with the advent in the globalization and capitalist monopoly this had also centered it's roots in different parts of the world in different societies. But this is not actually the thing through which we saw, "ideally homosexuality is very much natural as heterosexuality" and the answer of me being different is "being different is what makes all same" same as family and binds us with our uniqueness which helps us in overcoming the obstacles within a society.

From the very childhood of mine, I had seen people making fun out of my body language , the way I used to walk , I used to talk , my interests and specially my sense of belonging to a particular thing. ' due to all these circumstances somewhere in the bottom of my heart I also feel neglected and there was a time when I started judging my self and feels despicable about me'.

These situations becomes worse for me because I'm not defined " I didn't know where I have to stick to and whom gender I needs to feel attracted towards" there a incidence I was in my high school when I got attracted towards a boy who plays basketball in the school team, he is the head of the team and i always bunk my classes so as to see his game. One day the teacher saw me that I was out of class and watching the basketball match , she comes to me and sits next to me and asked me wheather I liked the game or want to play but with a way more innocence I directly told her that I always come to this field by bunking my classes so as to see the captain os the team. She was shocked , she went back to his room and called me after the break in her room so as to discuss all the matter of that playing and watching thing. I went to her room , the thing which I didn't like her to call me is "that I am a curse on my family and parents" that day I understand that being gay in a country like this where people of that country welcomes others with their open arms and full of life in their talks didn't have any space for a person like me not in their talks , in their arms and specially not in their hearts.

Being remembered in life is what all wants but if anybody is not having life then being in that is more important for the person then remembered. It's good to have traditions , and people with conservative mindset but it's not necessary that those people will then influence other's lives and choices and decides other people's way of living and the amount of respect and prosperity they hold. Many a times people got into a gay forward discussion that being straight is what our vedas and traditions had told us and it's our legacy to put forward the works which our ancestors had left for us{caste system} , basically being whatever whether a HIJRA , GAY , LESBIAN , BISEXUAL , QUEER OR HAVING SIDES is not in our control , many a times it's a person's personal choice of what thing excites him or her the most and according to that that person will then decides it's role , but such a concept generally occur in societies of open mindness , a society like of india where people never gave equal status to so called hetrosexual peoples also , there is a possibility of 0% till now to even gave equal respect to homo's within the block. Being traditional doesn't make a person to have all the privileges which a modern person with uniqueness in it's personality doesn't have.

It took me ten years to accept and respect my identity .

Today , saying this proudly that yes, I am gay makes me cry but then again makes me calm and quite because after all we are all part and linked to a society , where we are actually not the one who decides all about ourselves but it's the whole which decides our all………

Life is beautiful but not respectful neither workshipful………..

Its beautiful because I accept myself the way I really am , but its not respect full because the people doesn't accept me nor do they allow me freely express the opinions and liberal thoughts of mine.

I didn't have any choice but to accept myself before this society will going to , I never found myself guilty of what I had done in the past and what I am doing in the present but for me the guilty is the person {each person} who had ever in their life makes me down and didn't gave me opportunities to come at the surface , I am 21 just 21 and in this short span of life I had seen so much , had gone through so much that now I didn't either have the the potential nor the guts to lie anymore to anyone , I am tired of finding my space in this society , answering senseless questions , with discrimination , denied of even the basic necessities of life and the utmost important finding respect for me .

I had never feeled my childhood , nor I remember anything about my after age of it , the thing which I remember at the last is that I am a prostitute , gay , jobless , for society senseless , for government baseless and for family a black spot over their royal red respect , I always learn to pay back the society what we get from it but if there will be a time when the society wants the things back which they had given to me what should I give back them – ignorance , discrimination , baseless and senseless arguments just as to make their point of view correct , devoid of them separate sanitation rooms , housing , water facility , food security and most importantly not recognizing their identity .

Prostitution is not just a source of money for me but it's also a part of self identity for me because this is the only platform where my clients recognizes me with my sexuality and gets comfortable with it very easily. People always ask me to have a decent BPO job in the countrie's most metropolitan states but these multinational companies didn't accept me wearing heels and saying things a little loud and behaving feminine because with this there heterosexuality gets affected.

I choose prostitution because I am a sex addict also when you don't have anything to loose in life then you are one of the most dangerous creatures on the earth , this is what my story and "unsaid" is all about .

The field of selling myself on the roads starts for me when I was 16 years old , those were my high school days , I was not very feminine but a sex addict and this is the reason that I got into this business , it was the year 2012 I used to travel with metro from school to home and home to school , one day when I was waiting standing in the row of passengers for the metro to come I found a british boy standing next to me , he was continuously staring at me from the time of waiting to the arrival of the metro , this gave me an advantage over the discussion of asking that boy the reason for him to stare me , without wasting any more time I asked him his reason for staring at me , that boy very politely took my hand and asked me to come with him , at that time the thought of having sex with a white dick gravitate me towards that boy and I follow his instructions we both went out the metro station and from there we went to his rented apartment , when I was moving with him on the streets I was trying very hard to remember the areas and road lines from where we were going because many a times before this encounter I had been with some criminals as well who later after reaching their places had forcefully fucked me along with their friends who many a times came that place in between I was having coitus with the men who picked me up from the streets.

After reaching his apartment I found that the boy must be a film makers or a pornstar because when I entered his room I saw many cameras with naked men"s magazine along with dildos and vibrators , without any hesitation I asked him .

Are you a pornstar?

He didn't replied me as quickly and curiously as I asked him this question !

With this I asked him another question are you a filmstar or director ?

With this he starting explaining me about his life , he told me that he's gay paid pornstar and versatile ! with this I got stunned and asked me another question why you have so many cameras in your apartment and so many sex toys with you , do you make films ?

He nodded his head in a yes and then started undressing himself and after that undressed me , in between the kiss I saw him many a times looking at the camera and sometimes even setting it up towards our location , this makes me scared not because I afraid of cameras or don't have any plans to be in a porn movie but because that was too early for me to shine on a screen , I asked him of switching off the cameras and with this he did it very comfortably but at the final stage of his discharge he take a picture of mine with him in his phone and with it said to me of staying my night in his apartment but because it was already too late for me to stay in school for some work I left his apartment with some money which he gave to me by saying that this money if your charge which you had not demanded but I know that you needed and with this I was able to complete my first assignment where I took money and breed on a white dick.

For me prostitution starts from here because now I have a reason to do it with unknown persons in return of some benefits and cash and some memories which I got and had made with some special clients.

I never felt wrong when someone from the crowd came and say gay , meetha , chakka and fag to me because this is what they had learnt from this society , when I was in my college we didn't have any LGBT friendly society there when I demand for it the college administration declined it by using their veto powers over students matters that is just simply holding it and not giving any permission for it. A friend of mine who belongs to a very well educated family and his parents are serving in the union government once said to me that this homosexuality is a western concept and this is nothing to do with indian values and customs he even insisted of giving prove of it to me but my answer to him makes me a fun for him.

I simply said why aren't you taking then this westernized education go back to the veda ages where you will be founding manuscript and only the brahmins will be having the liberty to express and the whole society will then be divided into varna system just its prevelant in some other parts of the country even today , why are you wearing these westernized clothes and not kurta pajama and after that I even explained these things to him that I am not a supporter of western thinking but yes I am a follower of equal rights and humanity which we will specially the LGBTQ community will be getting after the introduction and through the better understanding of these modern westernized thoughts , these thoughts of mine doesn't sounds impressive to him and suddenly his patriotism level is above his head in which my rights have been drowned and then as usual he started teasing me for the way I walk , talk and specially debate , the problems became more hectic to me whenever I used to talk about LGBTQ rights with the NCC and military students , these students didn't want to understand such concepts and there was a time when I was explaining this to a person when homosexuality is not legal in the country {india} that because just for talking on this matter the men raped and abused me , now what reality presents in front of us now is that the men on the one hand opposed it and at the same time doing it "having sex with a men which the so called hetrosexuals had decided unnatural".

I always thought that the fight is just for behavior- like according to the norms decided by the society but this is a partial truth as things become large and I grew , I found this struggle is not just for behavior , claims , reservation or minority issues within the country for the community but the fight is for equality , liberty , justice , representation , and most important the fight for self identity .

When I came to know about me before anyone would know about it , I was not shocked but happy because when I didn't know about things , I felt neglected and deprived and this was the reason of mine degradation from a happy child to a prostitute , but after me knowing about myself I realize and felt liberated because now atleast I am defined that's the reason why there are so much more rape and sexually abuse cases with LGBTQIA+ people as compared to other people's including women's , because when a person is not defined and open for possibilities then it ultimately leads to abuse. if that person is not that much aware of it's consequences .and this the reason why in so many societies people easily accept their children's sexuality because they didn't want their life to get affected and don't want him/her to go through all such hardships and traumas.

Being a gay prostitute is not a really very easy task in a country like india where there is so much diversity and with this change in diversity at every step of country the pattern of society changes , there are areas within the country which are very much developed and whose nature of the society can be compared to the European societies at the same hand there are many more full fleged states within the country in which only the ruler had changed but the rule for the people remained exact the same as it was during the british time {opperesive and cruel} , with so much hardships within the work zone there you will be subject to so many abuses , threats and discrimination that if you are a gay men and sometime in your life traveled to such a place within the country with all your colours intact with you simply means along with your chaal dhal you will be going to convert yourself into a hetrosexual person either by hook or crook even if you don't have feelings for the opposite gender then also you have to marry in these backward areas with the opposite gender and this is know in india we got "mixed orientation marriages" and in china we got tongqi.

NON ACCEPTANCE

This is the last time I am meeting him. it's 2017, I know he loves me very much and so do I but the thing which is making me to leave him is NONACCEPTANCE { by the society}.

Starting of all these is just been a while, we met on a dating site because being GAY in a country like india is related to making yourself just loked in a closet where you can think about your desires and aspirations but there is no guarantee of making these true , nor by you neither by the society .

We talked almost about a month before planning to meet , he was very calm and responsive while chatting , I also took precautions because of mine past experiences , I was a student and he do business of cars , he had owned his own respect through his efforts in the business, nothing is hereditary given to him. We both are very much similar in habits, food choices, political discussions and this list becomes more long and wide when we starting dating each other. we usually talk about our carrers , family and past.

My past is not very good because at the age of 6 I was raped by my own uncle, then raped by many others of my own family , being a dalit I also faced discrimination in school even during my college admission process along with my father. His past is very much similar to me , the only difference between him and me is that I never gave on my studies and he quit it very easily , whenever we start such kind of a discussion he always said to me I want to see you in a car which have a beacon over it.{the OFFICER one}

Apart from our similarities , there is one thing which makes us differ from each other , the thing that he is getting married to a girl.

" And I will not marry to anybody"

There is no chance of a boy getting married to another boy with his own choice, till this stage of society's evolution when people have recognized the meaning of happiness not only in progressive societies but also in the developing societies, when this term is using by many political , economic scientists, and even countries leaders. then why don't they implement this on a ground level so as to make reforms in the society ,this dissision of me "not geeting married to anybody is not actually mine but imposed on me by the society because of the non acceptance they will make me face if I somehow in near future make myself married with a men of my choice".

Many a times I laugh very loud, and sometimes I started crying by looking at the situations which not only me aur any LGBTQ person is facing in our country but also the women's, unemployed persons,and people living under poverty lines are facing. the only thing which makes mine and other LGBTQ persons life more difficult is the judgement which people gave without even talking with us , they never want their childrens comes in contact with us nor do they like the way through which we as a person see the world .

He even invited me to his wedding , I also make my presence there .

After seeing me in front his weeding night , he starting crying and comes next to me and whispered me in my ears with his tears crawling onto his cheeks "let's get away from all this" we will make our own home where there is no society no opinions , nothing straight nor gay.

That time my whole body becomes cold and the only word which comes out from my mouth is there is no place like this. and we will never be one.

He pulled me towards him and starting crying more loudly , people attending that weeding looked us both very suspiciously , I said to him I am sorry we can't . and I left from his weeding , giving him a precious gift of the understanding of NONACCEPTANCE which I guess he will remember for life just I do remember it all time , all day and nights.

I really love him till this day when 377 is no more legal in the country , but now the difference is that he already have his own family. I met his daughter she is 1 year old and her eyes are very much like me, this time I met him in book fair , this time he again proposed me in front of his wife and want me to again come back to his life , but this time along with the nonacceptability, I even have another reason with it that's " I didn't want to ruin somebody's life when that life have responsibilities of another life" and most important I don't want to ruin her daughters future , just for my choices , the thought which every time comes to my mind whenever I look into this unsolved chapter of my past life is "MY NO - DUE TO SOCIETY'S NONACCEPTANCE AND HIS YES BECAUSE OF HIS COURAGE TO FIGHT WITH EVERYONE JUST TO HAVE ME THE ONE" MAY BE I AM THE COWARD……………………………………….

BETRAYED

When i was in my teenage days , I had came to know about a gay couple which were living just next to my apartment actually I had seen one of them always reading some sort of heavy books and the other men doing household works when these boys came to live in the apartment: they face many problems from the society staff , secretary , hetrosexual couples and most importantly from the orthodox priests and their followers of secular religions in the country. These problems became more and more turbulent when one of the society staff member notices one of the boy from the couple behaving differently usually like girls . but with all due efforts and making these boys paying more for the same size apartment as compared to the other couples , they got the apartment with some hard to remember points as a condition .

I first met the bottom guy when I was playing in the background of the building , there I found him sitting quietly under the peepal tree and looking at us with tears in his eyes , I didn't asked anything to him but went quietly towards him and with no emotion on my face and no hurry to listen his story sit next to him , at that point of time I didn't even realize that the men was not staring at us {the children} but actually there was a wedding happening next to the buildings mandir , everyone was laughing , children's were playing , traditional Indians wedding songs were played first on d.j so as to make the guests dance and then some of the not so popular had been sung by the families women's and I'm sure that this must be the men's reason to cry in silent , after 2 years of this gay couple living next to my apartment one day I came to know that the men who must be a top in this relation got selected in indian civil services . I found a ray of hope on the faces of both these men's that maybe now there voices must be heard by the government and judiciary……….. but now after me coming to the age of the bottom men when saw that top men with a women and children's came to realize the mistake which that bottom men had done for himself .

This is the year 2018: the year when I joined an non governmental organization named basic foundation basically this organization works for the LGBTQ+ society peoples and promotes safe men to men sex by providing assistance in forms of condoms and hiv testing free of cost within the nearby location of the organizational setup , when I joined this

NGO I didn't tell about this anyone in my family because of the prejudice linked with the community in the country but within one week I told my father about my work by thinking that maybe he will understand me and my work but the first expression which came from him was to leave the job and search for a more decent and stabilized job so as to easily get married to a middle class girl of the countries center but just like I always do I reject his proposal and said to him that I will surely leave the organization when I will find equality with dignity and specially marriage rights for the same sex couples within the country. This angered my parents and specially my father which resulted to a tight and hard slap to me from his side and with this I continued working in the NGO...

That was the month of august and me as an out reach worker was as always busy in distributing condoms to the needy prostitutes of the transgender and gay community peoples , but that day was not like the same as other days because when that day I went to the laal mandi {prostitute market}so as to distribute condoms and lubricating jellies to the community peoples , I saw a men aged around my father 40-45 sitting under a tree and relaxing , he was not looking and giving attention to any of the prostitutes and nor these sex workers asking him to anything in a gesture of respect or maybe these beautiful women's know him , at that time it was really shocking for me that in a lane where people specially men's came in a hurry with faces looking down on the ground so that no other men will be able to know their identity and after getting their sex done leaves in an more speedy way as compared to their prior coming there , this men was relaxing with his head high so that all the travelers in the lane will be able to look at his face but this showing off the face by the men makes me curious to know more about his story and his reason to making all the people's and travelers to look at his face , when I went to the spot where this men was relaxing I found his face similar to the gay couple bottom who used to live next to my apartment by around 15 years earlier.

When I went more close to him , I got tears in my eyes because the men by looking at my face hugged me tightly and without even realizing that he was having shortness of breath started asking me for his boyfriend , first I thought of not replying anything to him because upto this point of time also I didn't was very sure about that men's identity but when he grabed my hand and took me to a slum building where that men used to live from around 10 years now and showed me the potrait's which he make of his top partner and making me realize that the bottom is none other than the gay couple bottom , I started crying with him we both were crying by looking at each others face , I was not sure and was not having any knowledge so to what really happened to that men which made him degrade to such extent as he started living in the slumps and sleeping on the roads with his head high so as to make people remember him.

After weeping 15 minutes we both stand from our positions and I told him that I was leaving because I have some urgent assignments to complete , he pulled me close to him and in a very soft sound asked me to stay this night with him because he wants to share something really important of his life which he was not been able to make his boyfriend understand when they were dating each other , with this invitation and the curiosity to know what actually happened with this couple and most importantly with the bottom guy I accepted the invitation and called my parents that this night I will be staying with my college friends so as to make an urgent report on seismic activities at the mantle , when I was talking with my parents on my phone I saw him desperate to talk and share with someone by looking at a fake smile on his face and making his eye lashes up and down and due to this I didn't even making my parents to know my location quickly cut the call and put my bag filled with condoms and lubricating jellies aside from the bed in the room and sit on a chair which was near to the entrance of the room .

After giving him a small introduction about myself so as to remember him who am I and with this on my introduction he started laughing and said to me that he remembers everything and with this he even asked me that whether at that age I was thinking of having sex with him ?

Actually he was right , when I was in my teenage days and I saw him for the first time on his way to lift for the apartment , he was looking damn sexy in his short pants and full kurta , he always looks different because of his sense of styling from the rest of the colony people and many a times this sense of different looking became a key of teasing for him.

But of this question of his , with a big smile on my face I nodded my head in a no!.

So, I asked him to start telling me about his boyfriend , actually the reality was "that I didn't even remember the couple name also and wants *the narrator to start the story with the introduction including some of the minute details like name in it".*

He got up from his chair and went towards the kitchen and started making tea by reading a book , this thing sounds very funny to me because what I thought at that time was that "how could an indian men didn't know to make tea by having the fact that it's a kind'a national beverage for the whole country except some parts of south india" so without making any sense I asked him .

Didn't you know how to make tea ?

With this after loosing all ingredients into the bowl of tea making , he came to me and said this is how it all started . when he said this to me I saw some kind'a sadness on his face but because now I got indulged into the story I want him to tell the whole story with in the night without any serious breaks like emotional drama and crying.

I directly asked him seriously , with tea making your affair started ?

He again gave me that strange smile and nodded his head in a yes , with this I asked him to elaborate . and he started , he started the topic by introducing him to me with the name of Samarth and the top men as rajesh , he told me that when he { Samarth } was in his teenage days and was in high school , he used to stare rajesh because according to him rajesh was one of the most handsome brown boys of the school time and every girl wants to be in a relationship with him but rajesh was not good in studies as he was in sports and this is how Samarth got the plus point to initiate the conversation with him in the class , one day when the teacher was distributing their unit tests , the teacher shouted rajesh's name with a hard tone which create noise in the whole class and wants him to go out of the class so as to talk with him in private , the whole class was laughing on him but not me {Samarth} , when he got out of the class and after 30 minutes the class was over I went towards his bag and since that was the recess time everyone in the class was having their brunch and I was the only one who was completing his Sanskrit homework so in the next period the teacher will not shout on him again ;......

With this I asked him that are you serious that you were doing rajesh's homework and no one in the class notices you? With this he gave me a smile and said to me don't interrupt I am in flow, and on this we both laughed loudly.

On my question then he said that he was doing it secretly without anyone's noticing it, I halfheartedly agreed and with an ummm wants him to continue the story, so when the time of another class started I went on my chair with very fastly completing his homework and when the teacher started checking our notebooks she got very surprised by for the very first time seeing rajesh's homework completed, and this is how with a great surprise for the Sanskrit teacher the school ended that day, he then told me that suddenly when he got back his home and having his snacks he got a call on his landline no. as usual i{Samarth} ignored it but when it rang so many times that it became uncomfortable for me to focus on my reading magazines, I took it and there I found my crush on the other side of the call, first he thanked me and said to me that he knew that his work was completed by me and when I was cutting the call with saying byee and its ok, he eventually said why don't you come at my place for a tea in this evening.

and with this listening to him me{harsh "listener"} I gave him a smile and said ok tell me what happened that evening as if I already know that he accepted that invitation. With this he said to me by bringing the tea from the kitchen that now you know the beginning.

When we were quietly having the tea, I was looking at his face "pale, dark, and full of emotions", in that quiet moment I make the sound by asking him, did your parents know about you both?

what's their reaction when they came to know about your and rajesh's sexuality?

When and how they came to know about your relation with him?

Why you started living here alone?

What happened with rajesh now?

Where is your family now and are you in touch with them?

With these instant questions he gave a kiss on my cheeks and said to me wait kiddo. I will tell everything to you and with this I smiled and quickly finished my tea giving him a gesture of curiosity to know more about him
.

He again started talking but now in a standing position by repeating my first question to him ! he said yes my parents know about me but rajesh parents didn't know about him because actually rajesh is not gay but bisexual and when he said this. without even listening to the whole sentence I said in a very calmy voice "that's why I saw him with a women and a children"by listening this that bottom guy became curious to now know about him from me , he started asking questions to me just like I was doing some times earlier to him!

He asked : where you see him?

Did he have baby boy or girl ?

Is he lives near you and how many members are there in his family now?

With such unexpected questions from him , I somewhere knew that from his 2nd question that his ex boyfriend got married in front of him only.

I somehow managed him by saying will surely tell you everything about him what I know but after your story , with this he started saying things fast like when he and I was going out for studies we rented your buildings apartment and there we for the very first time had done it but we were in love with each other from the school days and this love became more and more intense when we live in together.

after saying this to me he suddenly becames mum and now I know his voice was chocked because he was controlling his tears and emotions both at the same time. With this I didn't ask much to him but a last question : why are you here and who is responsible for this state of yours ?

he again smiled and went outside to his room , I didn't followed because I know that time he just need himself , after 10 minutes later he came again and asked me a question : have you ever heard of drain of wealth theory ?

I said : ya

Did u know what kind of economic situation we had when britisher's left our country ?

I said: yes

Have you ever heard of famines during the british time in india?

Again yes.

Had you ever heard of partition stories and how did it affect so many Indians life?

Again yes.

I asked what does theif's country{united kingdom} had to done with your story?

He replied : I took myself as india and rajesh as the theif country UK. !

This doesn't sound impressive to me at all and so I directly asked him did he had taken your property and left you here in poverty stricken camps and brothel's. with this he said by crying with sounds that rajesh sold him there for 20,000 rs/- to a transgender women and with this without believing on this statement of his I said to him.

Now you are lying to me because an post graduate men like you on this I stopped and said how can someone do this to anybody whom he love? I started crying with him and we both again sit on different sides of the room started crying loudly and looking at each others face. When we were crying I got some other different sounds as well from the upper rooms of the buildings too , some of moaning , some of crying and some of laughing , with this I sit next to Samarth and asked him what was happening upstairs?

He said it's a daily routine here , and the most impressive thing is no one is here to judge you and sell you because we all had our rate tags attached with us .

Now it's 8 in the night and I thought that Samarth will going to tell me his story last stage suspence of why his lover sold him to this market where you have no value for love and respect for genders basically it's a genderless sex market what people need here is either bun or bread. But I was wrong because now it's his time for work , he got up gave me a 50 rs/- note , kissed on my forhead and whispered in my ears "will see you soon".

With this I also stand from my spot took all my things from there and kissed samarth's forehead and said to him will surely meet in future .

But it's been 3 years now , I saw rajesh everyday because he had left his A grade service and now works for social cause like making people aware about government policies and works with MGNREGA farmers but whatever cause now he will done for poor farmers and people's he will never be able to return the same life to Samarth nor his self esteem which rajesh had crushed some 15 years past.

Now I left it to the readers what perspective they made for Samarth : whether a betrayed homosexual indian men , prostitute , dumb. and what perspective they made for rajesh :betrayer , exploiter , men with double standard's or.....

STRUGGLE TO COUNT

Life never remains the same when any kind of incident happens with someone , but that incident always makes the victim more unhelpful and an easy target. That incident can be of any kind and it's degree and rate of trauma faced by the victim varies from societies to societies world over.

After getting raped and assaulted many a times with many persons , I became an easy target of people specially: boys and men's living nearby me. They used to call me with different names , any person easily in front of my relatives and family members comes next to me and badly touches me and if anytime , I shout they threatens me that they will going to tell everything about me to my parents and this is how then I make the things go along with the flow.

Whenever i tell my story to anybody specially: boys and men's of all ages, that person also make me mention his name too in the list of those whose stories I can't tell to anybody. This is not the only struggle which I am facing till this date of my life but there are many which somehow I had already faced and some which I am facing right now also. One of the most important count from all experiences is of "REALISING MINE

OWN INTEREST" here the subject becames more wider because interest here is not relating to culture or habits but my own WAY TO CHOOSE & LIVE , SEXUALITY , and somehow due to not getting the acceptance from people,{ this way of living , looking , and perceiving through my own lens of life's understanding becomes my religion and my culture}.

Things are very obscure for me till this time as well , as finding yourself different from the so called natural is a little hurtful , but a more shockfull when you realise and come to know that laws which are to mean for everybody doesn't have any provision for you and the only reason for this is your sexuality , that's your choice , your perception , your way of living and looking.

Usually we always comes to terms like : gender and many a times along with it's definition that it's a concept created by the society but never comes with terms like sexuality " in my opinion sexuality is a individual's personal choice of looking himself or herself and the kind of pleasure he/she wants to or wishes to have" these choices are dynamic as the lives , living standerds , and aspirations of people's are dynamic. {currently in gay's only we have top , bottom , versatile , cross dressers , and sides } these are more dynamic if we look at the societies of the west.

The first struggle which not every person in the society faces is his identification , the problem is not that I don't have any identification of mine but the one which I have is not meant for me actually. The first and the foremost struggle of mine to count is to find my identity who am I , why my interests are different from other boys , why I don't like to dress in a defined style created by taking into consideration some specified norms of the society , why things are more difficult for me rather other boys , why after using me specially boys and men's of different ages treated me and through me as if I am a polluting source , why people want me to clap and at the same time make fun of mine , why others is my status instead of not being a transgender , why people want me to be their sex slave , why people don't want to give me my rights , why there are no rites for marring the same gender under the directions and terms of society , why people don't want me to be a writer aur administrator "the fact is I don't know _but why their attitude towards me is like this , I don't know". After getting molested several times with several persons nearby me- somewhere in my heart I accepted this molestation as my fate my karma and many a times I even thought that all childrens go through the same suffering with whom I was going , but somewhere I know that *this is not the right way to think and understand what your karma have really set for you , being a buddhist i always learned to make yourself happy and through this you will satisfy your inner peace and now after so long of all that suffering I understand that this thought is the only reason for me to get into other dirty stuff and to come over with all those trauma's and mis-fortunes which somehow happened with me and became a part of my life and integral part.*

At the age of 14 when students of my batch in the school were talking of girls , modals , actresses I was talking of revolution "revolution in sex" this might look crazy to people who had only seen a one facet side of the understanding or reality and also because talking of sex in societies where people murder each other in the name religion , raped women's in the name of nirvana and follow unrealistic rituals just to satisfy their mental chemicals. There is no boy in any country who had not done his early sex with a men or a trans or a person who is gender neutral , I know this because in my school days I got many proposals from my own classmates of having done {sex}with them and they usually approach me because they want to explore more pleasure and something new most of times I got dirty proposals just because the other person is a virgin and wants to sealed it out , I handled all these in a very mature manner because at that time I was talking of revolution in sex , I am not saying or confirming that I was working as a kind of sex preacher but yes my motive is very much like that because I want to have space in that region where I was treated like an area .

All these incidents and encounters with males of different understanding and nature of their believe in equality had created opportunities for me to explore. My struggle to identify myself starts from here only , the simplest wat through which I came across to myself was not actually that much simple , from the very beginning of the chapters of discrimination I understood that I was not the same as other were and then slowly I understood not everyone is similar to others but then progressively with the getting of titles from other students and members of my own family I understood that I was again separated from that particular caste with whom I belong and the just reason for that is nothing but yes there are some superficial reasons which leads my excludation from that family also and those reasons are that superficial that even sometimes I gave a thought on them and feels neglected and shamefull .

My journey of identifying have just began because with the realizing of responsibilities and then shouldring them , a person understands his value and role in the different spheres which then leads to his widening of knowledge and then spreadness of that , my possibility of exploring myself have just started just like according to vedas a person have to suistain his life into 4 different spheres I thaught having a religion of humanity in myself my possibility of explorence of not only oneself but also others also got their relevance , making others understand what a person like me thaught and then giving those words credibility means a lot not only to suistain my words only but also to gave a generalized view to others of my revolution to thinking and looking at the world. " just like after the verdict on 6th of september 2018 the supreme court of india stated in its verdict of decriminalizing same sex _ I AM WHAT I AM SO, TAKE ME AS I AM". I not only understand the point very well but at the same time understands the future problems coming along with that decision. The decision now lies wholly in the hands of society and their way of looking to LGBTQ persons , being a part and a proximate observer I am writing this with the help of my newly gained rights that this change will not come in one night or day or under any pressure of supreme court guidance because after so many years of criminalizing any sort of untouchability within the nation , there are cases not several but many , after abolition of sati and child marriage there are people who are performing these rites my parents were married when they both were just 5 my parents didn't have any year gap between them . the observation which I got is that the people who practice and are in the forfront of making these practices sacred upto now are from the lowest level of society but contributes around half of the population these people are not having unity within themselves and that's the reason inspite of having democracy within the 7th largest nation in terms of size and 2nd largest nation in terms of population they didn't have been able to have their own leaders which will take their aspirations further and increase their level of accessibility of material resources.

I didn't object the way things are going into the society but I object the system where there is a huge population who have nothing and there are few who don't want to give anything to that huge mass , my situation here is in the in between's I was also objected and still people object the way I ask for things , write for rights , say on religion , and most important search for possibilities and quest for oneself but the thing which makes me and other LGBTQ persons differ from those of the huge is our *freedom of expression, what's the use of this democracy if people don't express their anguish, dissatisfaction, care, and patriotism in the way they were thaught to use it.*

Every person have sides, whether that person is a hetrosexual, homosexuals, have sides, gender neutral or whatever he/she loves to practice and wants to looks like, people generally refer to homosexuals in india as ardhnareshwar "having humanity first in heart" I don't care and even didn't listen what people say a community who is that much old as of first flourishing civilizations and here now I took the point of view "the stronger will suistain and survive and the weaker one will excluded from the chain or were treated as the subordinates just the aryan's treated the dasyu's and the white treated the blacks, this concept can be easily applied to understand the situation of gay people's in india, because of not having proper resources at the same time excluded from the family and became the sin on to the family by having of a particular sexual orientation or not accepting the norms set up the society or by having a different outlook from others or having same sex partner all this leads to making a person weak and the others hetro's then automatically became strong to survive in the environment of competition. what we got after revealing the whole secretive life which we were living is just fakeness from the society and even with the loved ones of ours, life can't be lived alone peacefully and joyfully but what about us we don't have our loved ones, we don't society, we don't have partners neither we got chances of adoption and that's why now if we need to change the scene and situations it's with these new constructed and given rights along with the rising of mental level of society, the shifting of power from the higher to the lower and the breaking of these orthodox, unrealistic, and superficial world of indian's which then only makes other to sustain according to the real nature of constitutional democracy within the country. and again as I always said "being diversified or different is not our weakness but being different is what makes us all same, a family and now after realizing this becomes our positive mould to give shape to a new, just and equalitarian society".

SYED

Things become so much complicated when nobody gave's you a reason to do that , this is the first time when anything like such happened to me . just for having a change from my daily boring works 'that day I make an account in the gay escort website of india.

my reason of making that account is very much like the things which I love to do , meeting new and handsome guys , come to know new and interesting stories about the people with whom I met and having a good time , I had never been to that website for selling myself.

Apart from grindr , in india gay men's don't have any other option to find their MR. RIGHT because being gay in a country with so much diversity is very challenging . this is my daily routine whenever I go to a hospital or any governmental or private organization's even in the local buses I have to make people understand that I am not different from them , it's just a matter of choices and its easy for them to accept gay's also because of their understandings of diversity and unity.

It's just half an hour of me making account on that website that so many proposals come to my inbox. i read each and every inbox message but one men which attracts me the most is syed , he was continuously sending me questions like: your name ?

Where are you from?

Want to meet you ?

Very curious for your reply's ?

Are you free today?

I think you are not interested ?

After seeing this much curiosity about me, I replied him," yes I am free today and love to talk to you." he very fastly replied.

your number?

It's also really becoming very hard and tense for me so as to operate on that website because it crashes several a times I guess so many people were operating it at the same time and this must be the reason of the crashing of the website.

I gave him my number but in one condition that he will going to pay me for my services and this made him agree to call me directly, I thought earlier before he called me, that he must treat me as an escort but what's his fault after all I am the one who gave him this offer of charging for my services. When he called me he talk like a gentle men, after a little normal conversation he directly started providing me with directions towards his house the mind map which I was making was actually new to me because earlier I never travel to chattarpur { A location in delhi} since the fact it is far near to my place, he gave me directions like from where and which metro station I have to deboard and then from there which cab should I take so as to reach his place, I listened all this very carefully and told him whenever I will be facing problem to reach his place I will call him and this then reach an aggrement, the aggrement also mentiones the amount which he will be giving to me, but this aggrement doesn't mentiones whether he will using condom or not when he will going to fuck me.

As according to the instructions provided to me by my client of the day I do the required and necessary, basically when I was travelling to his place from my college I even thought this that why am I doing this and what will be the result of this but the reality is two-folded I was doing it because firstly : I need money so to spare it on my college expence's because at this point of age I really feel awkward to always took money from the parents and secondly I was really looking forward to some adventure and as upto now the reader will come to know that I was addicted and horny all the time.

I reached the place as the time he mentioned, he wants me to come at the evening at 4 :00 at his place because I guess he must be an employee in and multi national company or what we mostly pronounce as an KPO knowledge processing outsourcing firm situated in Noida or Gurgaon, when I reached his place I called him , the area is not very posh as most places in delhi are and mostly in GK and chattarpur areas but there were high rise buildings over there.

some have metallic hard and solid beautifully written name plates over them of the business for which they are operating and others are just the resisdential apartments of either the employees or students the area is actually full of smoke coming out of industries situated near to that areas and next to those high rised buildings .

I found that my clients apartment is in the tenth floor of the building I took the lift as it will be really convienient and time saving for both of us , when I reached the tenth floor I found this area of the building very calm as if no one lives here or people are so busy that they didn't even want the other person living next to them to have their presence but what's my reasoning do with it I am here to work.

this is what I thought , I rang the door bell of flat no. 10/55 and got no response in the first attempt I thought whether I was get fooled by the client or whether I was in the wrong wing but after cross checking all the required information which the client gave to me I again rang the door bell this time also I didn't got any response so I thought of just waiting for 5 more minutes and then leaving the place actually in those 5 minutes I was criticizing and abusing that client because this meeting only leads to my money loss because I travelled to and forth without even getting my money back {travelling expences}.

When I was about to leave I found the lift getting open first I thought of asking the men coming from the lift about syed named person but before I could say anything to that person on the lift I found the person next to the first person in the lift is syed and this relaxed me because now atleast I will be getting my payment and I don't have to incur all the losses of my travelling , he came to me and hugged me and in a hurry opened the door and welcomed me I found it very surprising that he was also entertaining another boy on which he was next in the lift and from whom I was about to ask his name and address.

We three went in the apartment and then syed offered both of us soft drinks I appreciate the way he behaves with gay boys actually the reality in india for gay boys is quite harsh and uncivilized because people after taking their services or in general sense after taking advantages from them just threw them like chewing gums and which really can scare a person for life.

After having our drinks I told syed to start, he strated un clothing himself and then I saw the boy sitting next to me also started getting away from his clothes slowly slowly,

I found it disguisting and feel cheated because he was paying me only to having sex with him and not for 2 men's I very quickly announce my disappointment about that threesome I told the 2 of the present there that I will not going to do anything because syed had paid me for having sex with him and not for his friend also, with this syed came to me and gave me a tip of double the amount he was paying me for having it with him and then whispered in my ears is it fine now or you need some more.

At the same time he also announced that he don't like escort services with tantrums and now wished from me some better pleasure because afterall now he's paying more the amount he was earlier giving to me.

The sex was really nice afterall it's my first time threesome but I didn't like syed performance because he just laid down and wants both of us to explore every possibilities and curves of his giant tall body, syed didn't use condom and because it is dark I get myself sided and let syed fuck the other boy hardly, the boy takes all his cum in his ass and started moaning with cry because as I can understand its really hard for anyperson in this world for having a muslim dick fully in the men's pussy.

after getting done with the sex, I started clothing myself because now I have to submit my assignment in the college and because I was the very bright student the teacher didn't want me to get late in submitting my assignments because they thought me as the very calm, quite and innocent student of the college and this image really helps me in getting good marks in my internals because at the end of the day what my friend told me the image shines not the mentality " I found it gross because this mentality makes us slave of the british because"

"the emperor Aurangzeb saw their image but not their mental potentiality" but now the era have come to an end I found both of them still together kissing and licking each other penis till now.

After done with the clothing and getting my money share from the table I left the apartment and took the lift then a cab and then metro finally reached college submitted assignment and then buyed some novels which I was really looking forward to read from the money I get from the services I provided to the client named syed.

I thought it came to an end after the service because I even deleted my account from that website but soon after I found I started getting many calls from unknown numbers first I thought that the clients must have taken the number before of mine deleting the account but when I answer some of the calls in greed of getting some more work which have pleasure in it I found one of my family member talking to me and wants to have sex with me in an arrangement that otherwise he will gonna tell the whole narrative of me having an account in that website and even letting my parents know about my sexuality this is the same time when we don't have 377 decriminalised in the country ,

because of the reason that I had already deleted the account I didn't found his calls to tell my parents appropriate for that I will be having sex with him, I in a harsh tone told him to tell everything to my parents but at the same time I even tell him to have some prove with him whenever he will be narrating this to everyone in the family , he became silent and I cut the call.

After two weeks:

I again got call from syed , he told me that he was really looking forward to take me out for a date, I found it surprising that a men once a client of mine wants me to take on a date.

first I thought of refusing it but then I fixed it when he said that he will be going to pay for it the same amount which he had earlier given to me the day when I entertain him with the other boy , he told me of getting dressed in some feminine clothes so that no one outside the hotel or the place wherever we will be going notices us but this demand of the client creates difficulty for me because now how will I going to dress in feminine clothes in my own house when no one in the family and building knows about my sexuality and work apart from that creep family member who wants me on his bed . I decided 3 things to get prepared for the date.

1.to get some clothes but from where will I getting clothes ? so for that I took the way towards madhav's house tell him everything and took some of his well feminine clothes and an artificial hair wig from him now when I get all my dressing.

Then I went for the:

2. makeup which madhav had done but not in his house because then that will be problematic for both of us to go out with it on my face its normal for madhav to be infront of everyone what he actually is but its not same for me or anyother person who still lives in the closet.

3. then i get dressed which also madhav had done to me he really have a great sense of fashion we went to the nearby city walk mall and in the bathroom of the building we dressed in a queen's dress and by we I actually mean madhav too because this is the first time when I was getting dressed in such clothes and what if someone when I go for the date start teasing me what if the police will rape me as always happens with the LGBT in the metropolitan city , when we need help in metropolitan cities like delhi no one cames forward but whenever they saw people like us there you will find crowd of people wasting their time and money just to see the people's .

Now after all that stuff I contacted syed he wants me to come to the lalit kitty su which is the most liberal place for all kinds of persons in the city I had heard about it very much but never went to there because it's too expensive to have it's experience but madhav once in a month always went there , we both went towards the road so as to having a cab but then we both decided to go by the metro because we both wants to flaunt our queerness and make others see rainbow love in the air.

When we reached the metro station we found things really troubling for us because there we don't have cheaking counters for LGBT there you will found only 2 cheaking counters male and female we both went in the male counter there the police personal didn't allowed us to went ahead and suggested us to go in the female counter when we went there the female cop shouted in fear and didn't allow us to went for the ride then we both went towards the office headquarter.

first the officer gave both us a sharp and shrink look as if we were there to make his son marry with both of us but when we told all this to him he called the ground staff and scolded all the police personals first who didn't allowed us to enter and second who shouted in fear after this he say sorry to us and also mentioned that please don't write a letter to the chief minister of the NCT about our behavior at that point of time we understand why it's really important to have democracy in the country.

We both deborded at cannught place metro station and from there took a walk to the kitty su hotel when we went inside the hotel there we found mostly uncoloured people we mean by it the whites there we didn't find any brown men and women then one men came and offered both of us drinks that person is none other than syed , we both went for the drinks and started chatting about madhav he asked him whether he is a trangender or gay he sidelined himself by saying he is a great human being who give smile and pleasure to people like him , this made me laugh and syed cough , then all three of us went to the dance floor and started dirty dancing because there was no one in the club to judge us.

we went ahead more than dancing syed and I started kissing , madhav joined us later after finishing his dance moves and then after spending 4 hours in the club he proposed me , madhav was astonished and so do I first I took it lightly and said yes then when madhav told me that he was really serious about it I told him not to do any such thing again with me , he nodded in a yes and then we went towards the food counter .

It's now 8 in the late night evening and madhav wants me to go with him at his place but I resisted , madhav took me the side corner started making me getting rid of the dress and heels told me that how difficult it is to boy's like us have someone to love in their life not only in india but all around the world , I took his advice and tell syed to book a cab from here to his place first he thought of that madhav was going with us but with an eye gesture I told him that he is not going with us , he smiled at me and booked a cab from the entrance of the hotel it will took 15 minutes to reach the cab at the entrance then I started looking for a silent corner in the hotel and called my papa{father} that I will be staying today in my friend's home for some urgent file work and assignments after getting his permission I called my mother and repeated the same lines and got her permission as well .

when the cab arrives we both left the hotel and went for his place and madhav travelled alone the whole way from cp to madangir.

When I entered his home he suddenly blindfolded me and this scared me I thought that he must be a seriel killer who will now taste my blood but when I resisted he grabed my hands tightly and switch on the lights and let my eyes and hands move freely when I in a hurry opened the eyes I was surprised because there I found a bath tub full of flowers and water milk in it and chocolates on the table , after seeing this I cried very loudly and he came next to me started kissing me and doing shhhh...

To me the moment was very romantic and that day I had experienced two different things which I had never experienced before when we were doing sex I saw his passionate side this time but after getting done with it I found that there was a picture of a women on the wall which looks very young I thought earlier of that women must be the sister of the men but when I asked with curiosity who she is ?

he started crying and with it in a non understandable voice started telling me the story he said she was her wife and one year earlier she was murdered , he even told me that now after one year of her demise her case is still open like a deadly mystry.

In the morning I went for my house took the cab and the metro and then an auto to reach my place , when I went to my house I found no one because both my sisters and my parents are working I took the shower have a tea called madhav to come and then after he came I distributed the amount which he gave to me as an service charge after money distribution I told him the whole story and then madhav wants me o have link with this person for life .

We both syed and I started talking to each other from the very next day of our kitty su meeting he always wants me to joins in his parties but with one condition that I will be dressing like a transgender he is more a transgender lover than a men lover but after that last night stay meeting I refused all these proposals of his because now I will be having m 5th semester exams which even includes dangerous practicals , I had already told him about it but he always used to knock at my phone with so many missed calls that somewhere I even realized that he is very much started behaving like a delhi lover who used to call their partners all the time , even wants to know the minutest of details around his surroundings and always plans for the weeding .

Somewhere I also liked it but as we know that all great things have an end .

One night I got a call from malviya nagar police station they wants me to be present there within an hour otherwise they will be charging me against some false cases. This is really hectic and unknown to me because earlier I had fucked some police personals but they never want me to be with them in the thana {office} I told my parents that I will be going to my nearby friend's house for studying and after getting permission "well at that time I didn't even mind to falsifying their permission if they didn't even get me" I called madhav he wants me to wait at the saket bus stop and after half an hour and so we both went to the police station and there when we tell a havildar that we got a call from the office he took us in the senior police office and by looking at us he directly asked madhav "kotti hai kya" madhav didn't say anything and I told him the story that I got a call from the department he asked me the mens name who called me but that time I was in a hurry I didn't able to ask his name I said to him he wants bots os us to wait outside and after some 10/20 minutes later he called us with an halvildar and suddenly what I found I was slapped by an women sitting opposite to the chair of the police officer .

I was blanked suddenly what she told me shocked me the most than any other thing on this earth she said she is the wife of syed and now syed is dead in her story I by listening this interrupted the women in a hurry and told her that I talk with syed almost everyday she told me that I am right but the reality is that syed got his death by an car accident which happened this night when I was talking with him and that's why the police make me come at the office .

the police men asked my rishta{realtion} with syed ?

I told him that we were good friends

Another question comes from the womens side : don't you think you and syed have age gap of about 12 years how you met her ?

I directly in a proximate manner told her that we both met on a friendship site and then we occasionaly met for drinks and parties.

Another havildar comes with all phone records between me and syed and then there were stroms of questions exchanged between me and her wife and then between me and the police men and then between me and the havildar , they didn't even want me to get some time for having water and then side by side many people started asking me questions.

many a times the policemen even slapped me and called me with different hindi LGBT slangs but this didn't made me accept what they were saying , after 2 hours of remand they left me with madhav and told *me of not going out of delhi and whenever they will be calling me I have to be there but from that day I didn't got any call from the police station nor from her wife , nor do I know whether now syed is dead or her wife .*

The one thing which I can say about this encounter is that it will remain alive forever with this book.

Manufactured by Amazon.ca
Bolton, ON

45855945R00032